NICHOLAS HELLER

Ogres! Ogres! Ogres!

A Feasting Frenzy from A to Z

Pictures by
JOS. A. SMITH

Greenwillow Books, New York

Goauche, watercolor paints, and watercolor pencils
were used for the full-color art.
The text type is Isbell.

Greenwillow Books, a division of William Morrow & Company, Inc.,
1350 Avenue of the Americas, New York, NY 10019.
www.williammorrow.com
Printed in Singapore by Tien Wah Press
First Edition 10 9 8 7 6 5 4 3 2 1

Library of Congress Cataloging-in-Publication Data

Heller, Nicholas.
Ogres! ogres! ogres!: a feasting frenzy from A to Z / by Nicholas Heller ;
illustrations by Jos. A. Smith.
p.   cm.
Summary: The letters of the alphabet are represented
by an assortment of ogres devouring all sorts of foods.
ISBN 0-688-16986-4 (trade).   ISBN 0-688-16987-2 (lib. bdg.)
[1. Ghouls and ogres—Fiction.   2. Food—Fiction.   3. Alphabet.]
I. Smith, Jos. A. (Joseph Anthony), (date) ill.
II. Title.   PZ7.H37426Oh   1999
(E)—dc21   98-51919   CIP   AC

For Maxine
—N.H.

This one is just for Charissa
—J. A. S.

Take a peek through the trap door.
What do you see?
Insatiable ogres feasting on
fabulous foods from A to Z.
Look!

Abednego adores anchovy butter,

and Beulah blows
bubbles in her chocolate.

Coralee consumes
cartons of dumplings,

and Dermot dispatches
deviled eggs.

While Esme enjoys
eggs flambéed,

Fergusen flips frogs' legs on the griddle.

Gabby gobbles gobs of hummus.

Hobart's hat is heaped
with ice cream.

Indolent **I**mogen
imbibes juices,

and jovial Jehosephat
juices kumquats.

Klangbourne knocks back key limes,

and Lagthorpe laps
ladles of molasses.

Melanie merrily
munches nuts,

and Nicodemus nibbles
numerous oysters.

Odelle opens olives to get the pimentos.

Pernilla is peppering
her parsnip quiche.

Queenie quaffs quantities of root beer.

Roscoe relishes
ripe strawberries.

Stanley swallows
succulent tangerines.

Tallulah tries to taste
the upside-down cake.

Una upends urns
of vichyssoise.

Voracious Vlad vanquishes
the watermelons,

while Wanda wolfs
waffles in excess.

Xavier is extremely excited over yogurt,

young Yusef yells,
"More zucchini!" and

Zuleika zips zealously
through her asparagus!

But be quiet while you're peeking.
Don't let the ogres hear!
If your tummy starts to rumble,
they all will disappear!